THE
SOUND
OF
SILENCE

By
**Katrina
Goldsaito**

Art by
Julia Kuo

L B

Little, Brown and Company
New York Boston

Little Yoshio wiggled with anticipation.

Three...two...one!

He threw open the front door.

The sounds of the city swirled all around him—
Tokyo was like a symphony hall!

Yoshio listened to the sound of his boots squishing and squashing through the puddles, and the tiny raindrops pattering on his umbrella. The sound of his giddy giggles made him giggle more.

Suddenly, Yoshio heard the strangest sound,
high and then low, squeaky and vibrating—
amazing! It was a koto player
carefully tuning her instrument.

Then the koto player played.
The notes were twangy
and twinkling; they tickled
Yoshio's ears! When the song finished,
Yoshio said, "Sensei, I love sounds,
but I've never heard a sound like that!"

The koto player laughed, and
it sounded like the metal bell
that swayed in the wind
in Mama's garden.

"Sensei," Yoshio said,
"do you have a favorite sound?"

"The most beautiful sound,"
the koto player said,
"is the sound of *ma*, of silence."

"Silence?" Yoshio asked.
But the koto player just smiled a
mysterious smile and went back to playing.

Yoshio bowed to the koto player and ran to school.
Where can I find silence? Yoshio wondered as he listened to
the thwack of his boots on the pavement.

He listened for it through the school day, but there was always some kid making noise. At recess, the sun came out and Yoshio went to the quietest place he knew— the bamboo grove at the edge of the playground. But even there, the bamboo made a *takeh-takeh-takeh* sound as the wind banged its stalks together. He closed his eyes and heard the *swish-swish-swish* of the wind making the leaves talk. It was beautiful, but it wasn't silence.

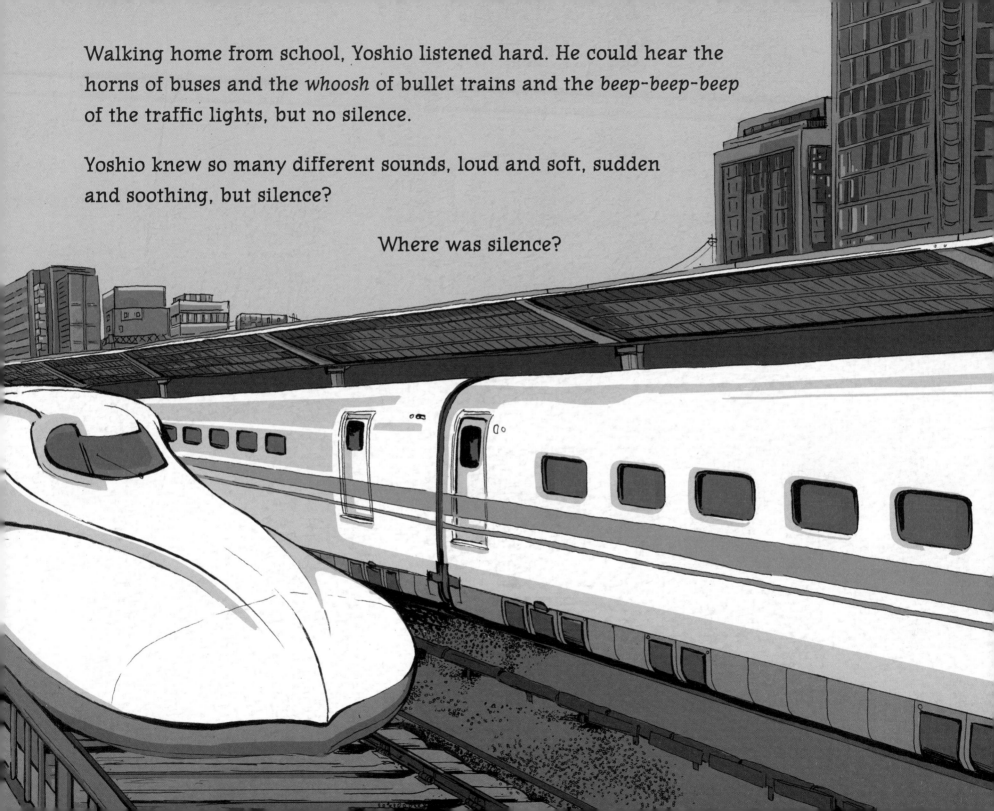

Walking home from school, Yoshio listened hard. He could hear the horns of buses and the *whoosh* of bullet trains and the *beep-beep-beep* of the traffic lights, but no silence.

Yoshio knew so many different sounds, loud and soft, sudden and soothing, but silence?

Where was silence?

It wasn't in the dining room, where there was always the sound
of chopsticks and slurping and chewing and swallowing.

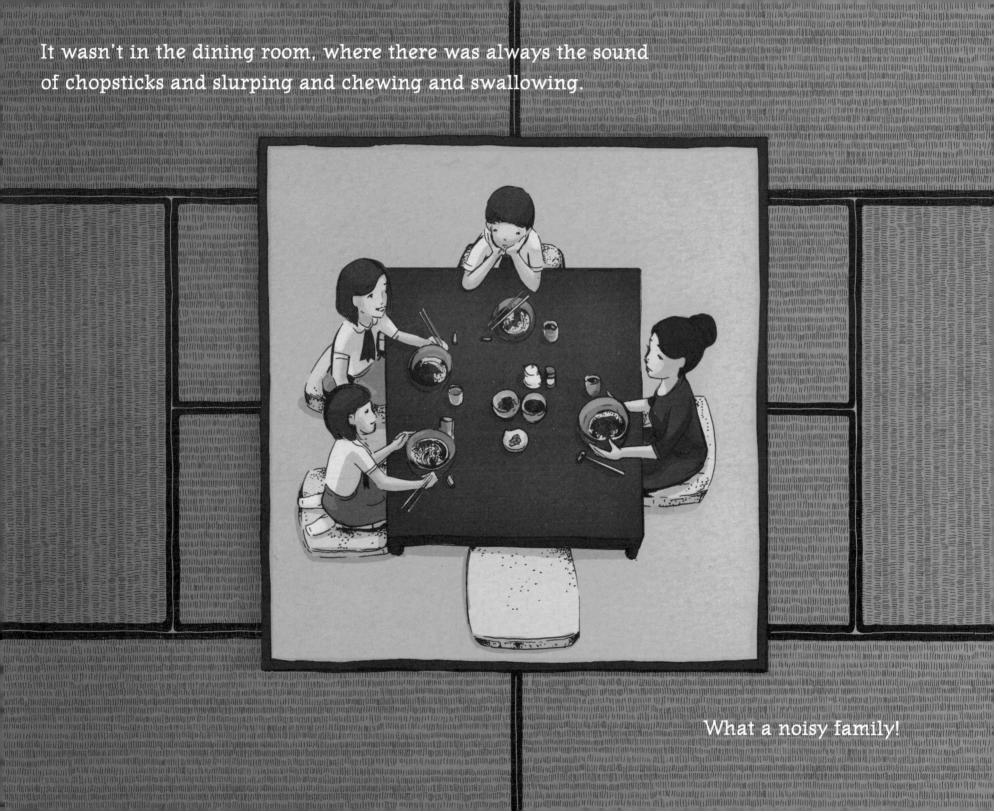

What a noisy family!

Silence wasn't in the bath, where even his toes made noise and little droplets of water kept dripping off his nose.

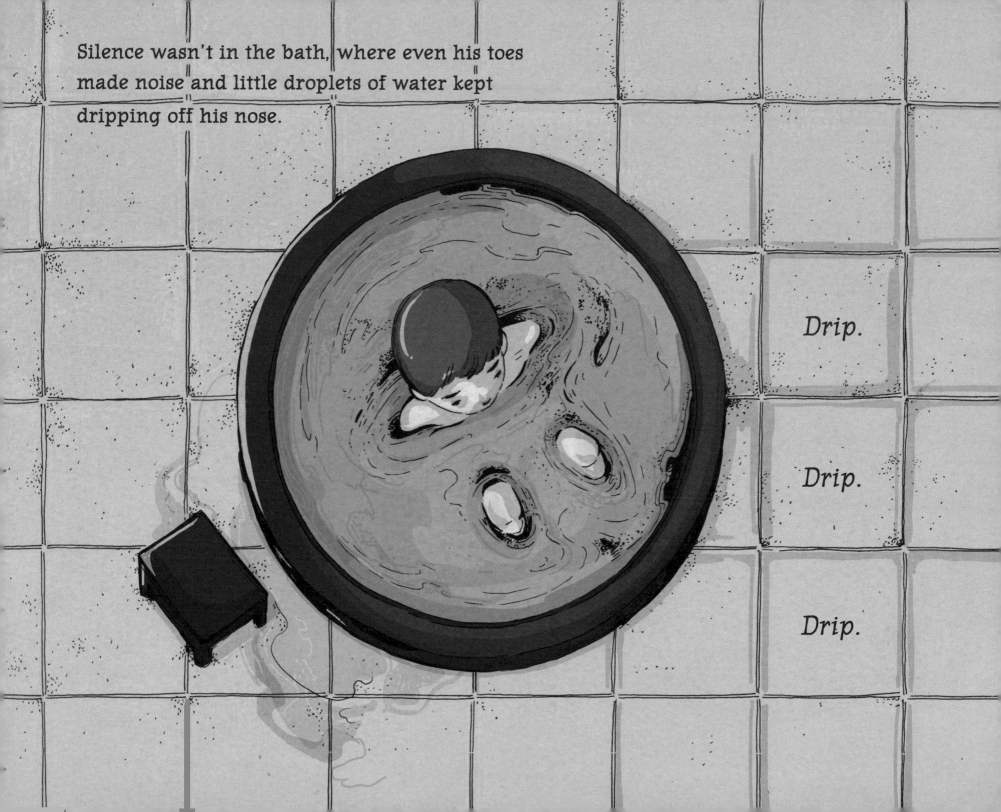

Drip.

Drip.

Drip.

That night, Yoshio tried to stay up late to catch the silence while his family slept.
But his eyes got heavy and then heavier, and soon the sound of a distant radio
became part of his dreams.

The next morning, Yoshio woke up to his
neighbor's dog barking and barking and—
oh no! He had missed the silence!

Yoshio walked to school early. His sisters whizzed by on their way to the park, screeching Yoshio's name.

Where was silence?

Yoshio heard the creak of the school gates as he pulled them open. No one was at school yet. He put on his inside shoes and listened as they shuffled on the shiny floor.

The classroom felt
different without anyone in it.
He sat at his desk by the window
and pulled out a book. He loved this story,
and as he read, he forgot where he was.

Suddenly, in the middle
of a page, he heard it.

No sounds of footsteps, no people chattering, no radios, no bamboo, no kotos being tuned.

In that short moment, Yoshio couldn't even hear the sound of his own breath.

Everything felt still inside him.
Peaceful, like the garden after it snowed.
Like feather-stuffed futons drying in the sun.

Silence had been there all along.

It had been there between the thumps of his boots when he ran; when the wind stopped for just a moment in the bamboo grove; at the end of his family's meal, when everyone was happy and full; after the water finished draining from his bath; before the koto player's music began—and hovering in the air, right after it ended.

It was between and underneath every sound.
And it had been there all along.

Ma,

silence.

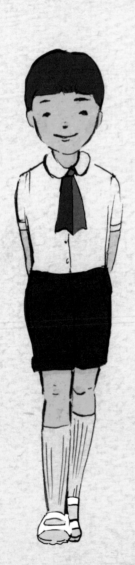

The Japanese concept of *ma* is the silence between sounds. It's the moment when musicians pause together, and is at the heart of traditional Japanese music, dance, tea ceremony, flower arrangement, storytelling, and even conversation!

Ma is a silence loved by contemporary Japanese composer Toru Takemitsu. He was well known for his compositions for film greats such as Akira Kurosawa and Masaki Kobayashi. He says that without silence, sound would be meaningless.

It was this very same composer who lived next door to my father when he was growing up in Tokyo. When my father asked the famous composer, "What is your favorite sound?" Toru Takemitsu answered that his two favorite sounds were "the wind through bamboo and the sound of silence."

Takemitsu was discovered by Igor Stravinsky and heavily influenced by John Cage, a composer who also loved silence. Takemitsu says in his book *Confronting Silence* that one day on the crowded Tokyo subway, he realized he must incorporate the sounds of the city into his compositions. He says that he wanted to give "meaning to that stream of sounds that penetrates the world we live in."

Tokyo's "stream of sounds" is what Yoshio loves. When I was a little girl, my father would teach us to meditate by listening to the sounds around us. After we finished he would ask, "How much time do you think has passed?" and we would never know if it had been five minutes or thirty. This elasticity of time as Yoshio appreciates all the sounds around him is part of the Zen goal of being in the moment.

In the end, the concept of ma is what Yoshio searches for and eventually finds, and ma is the silence that you, too, can find in the spaces between sounds.

—*Katrina Goldsaito*

Yoshio is a collector of sounds! You can search for them, too:

Zaa-zaa the gush of rain when it's pouring down.

Kiii the squeal of brakes when a car stops.

Pu-pu the honk of a car horn.

Buu buuuu the rumble of a car engine.

Takeh-takeh-takeh the sound I imagine when hollow bamboo stalks bump against each other. (*Take* is the word for bamboo.)

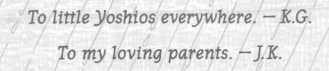

To little Yoshios everywhere. — K.G.

To my loving parents. — J.K.

ARTIST'S NOTE:

The illustrations in this book were drawn in pen, scanned, and colored digitally in Photoshop. This story is told around many bustling city scenes, and I thought it would be fun to make these backgrounds identifiable to people who are familiar with Tokyo. I drew on my own memories of Tokyo as a visitor and included my favorite Japanese companies, authors, and artists. I also thought about the time I've spent visiting my family's Taipei home from childhood to adulthood, and how my experiences of exploring the same city have changed as I've changed. I hope I can always find fresh new ways to observe and listen to the world like little Yoshio, no matter where I am!

—*Julia Kuo*

ABOUT THIS BOOK:

This book was edited by Bethany Strout and Alvina Ling and designed by Saho Fujii. The production was supervised by Erika Schwartz, and the production editor was Annie McDonnell. This book was printed on 140gsm Gold Sun woodfree. The text was set in Journal Text, and the display type was hand-lettered.